The S PARTY

Om
KIDZ
An imprint of Om Books International

Published in 2017 by

An imprint of Om Books International

Corporate & Editorial Office
A 12, Sector 64, Noida 201 301
Uttar Pradesh, India
Phone: +91 120 477 4100
Email: editorial@ombooks.com
Website: www.ombooksinternational.com

Sales Office
107, Ansari Road, Darya Ganj, New Delhi 110 002, India
Phone: +91 11 4000 9000, 2326 3363, 2326 5303
Fax: +91 11 2327 8091
Email: sales@ombooks.com
Website: www.ombooks.com

ISBN: 978-93-86108-21-0

Printed in India

10 9 8 7 6 5 4 3 2 1

The Surprise
PARTY

My name is

mayneha

Gia is a **toy** doll. It is **her** birthday. **But** no **one** remembers. **Gia** is very **sad**.

Gia lives in **Amy**'s cupboard. **Her** best friends **are Pip the toy dog**, **Ted the** teddy bear **and** Toto **the top**.

But the toys have not forgotten Gia's birthday. They are going to give Gia a fun surprise party.

"I will make a **jam** tart," says Toto.

"I will make a **pie**," says **Ted**.

"**And** I will make a **pot** of **tea**," says **Pip**.

Gia sits by **the** window, looking at **the sky**. It is a nice **day** outside **and the Sun** is shining. **She** sees a bird **fly** past. **But she** is still **sad**.

13

Suddenly, **she** hears **the** toys **say,**
"Happy Birthday **Gia!**" **She** looks
around. A **big** smile forms on **her lip**.

The toys have **set** up a table with **jam** tarts, a **pot** of **tea and** a **fat pie** that looks so **yum**. **And** of course, a **big**, **big** cake.

Gia claps **her** hands. **She** gives **the** toys a **big hug**. **She** is so happy that they remember **her** birthday. They **sit** at **the** table.

Gia sees a **big box** with a **red** ribbon on **the** table. **She** opens **the** box. There is a **new hat** in **the box**.

Gia jumps with **joy**. **She** loves **her** gift. **She** puts **the hat** on. **She** ties **the bow**. **She** looks at herself in **the** mirror. **Gia** looks nice.

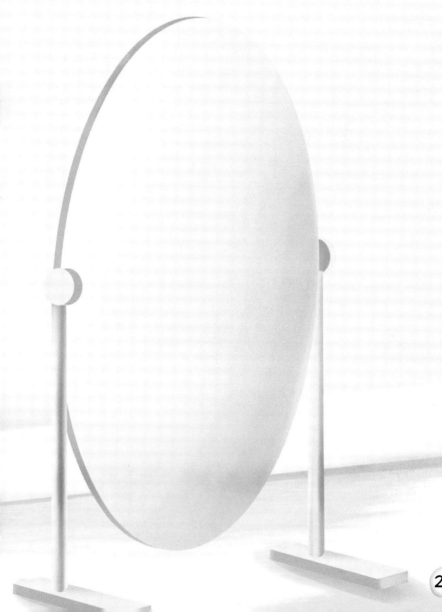

"**Let** us **cut the** cake," says **Pip**.
Gia cuts **the** cake **and** blows
out the candles. **She has** a
sip of **tea**.

The toys make popcorn.
It goes, "**Pop! Pop! Pop!**"
They **eat** a **lot** of tarts. They **hop**
around **and** have a **lot** of **fun**.

Now it is time to go to **bed**. **Gia has had** a lovely birthday. **She** gives **all the** toys a **big hug**. **She** is happy at last.

Match the words
to the pictures.

HAT •

PIE •

BOX •

TOP •

POT •

DOG •

Fill in the last letter to make the word.

T O   P I P   B O X

H A T   D O G   J A M

Find and colour the words with the correct crayon.

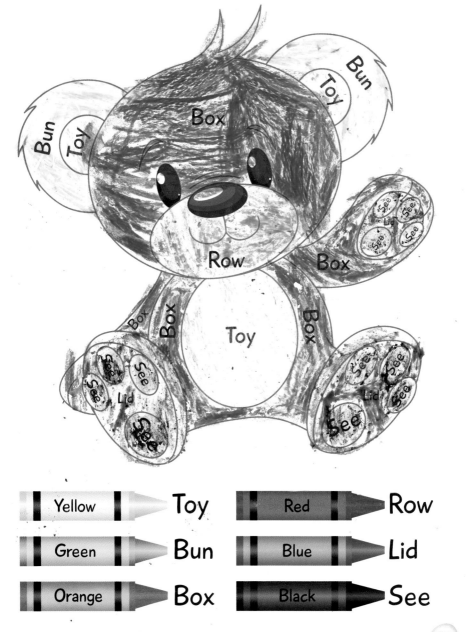

Yellow	Toy		Red	Row
Green	Bun		Blue	Lid
Orange	Box		Black	See

Know your words

Sight Words

but	fun	yum	has
one	lot	sit	had
her	day	red	all
are	sad	new	she
the	big	joy	pop
and	set	let	now
not	fat	sip	out

Naming Words

Gia	Ted	tea	hat
toy	top	sky	bow
Amy	jam	Sun	bed
Pip	pie	lip	
dog	pot	box	

Doing Words

eat	fly	hug
hop	say	cut